D1447103

CARLISLE
&
IVY

USA TODAY BESTSELLING AUTHOR

Nothing could hide her from me.

The darkness is everywhere and it moves about in the mortal realm....
And then there's her.
Bright and so easily seen.

Mine.

She calls to me like I prayed to the Gods she would.
I should feel guilt for what I'm going to do. What I must do.
She doesn't remember, but I do. She belongs to me.

I will claim her and bring her to the underworld as mine.
At all costs... nothing will keep me from what belongs to me.

A Deal For A Kiss

Prologue

Ivy

It was black for only a moment. In and out of it I went. Her voice was there; I was surrounded by the strangers on the street. It was plain and normal, and I had nothing to fear. Then there was nothing.

In a single step the chill of fall was gone. The heat licked across my back as if flames were there, but it was vacant of light. Nothing but darkness.

In a blink, the light returned. People moved about me as if nothing had happened. My heart rampaged, desperate to escape, and my scream was caught in the back of my throat.

Had it happened at all? Too paralyzed to move, all I did was breathe, then I was taken again. Back to the darkness, falling this time and landing harshly on the rough carved stone beneath me.

I could see nothing, feel nothing but the unforgiving stone. Hear nothing but the violent beat of my pulse. I thought there was no one and nothing, until I felt him behind me. Turning as quickly as I could served no purpose; there was nothing but blackness surrounding me.

Surely I was somewhere I didn't belong and then, at once, I was returned. Back to the modern world built on ancient ruins with a history so cursed and intricate not a soul could know of what would plague me. Of him. I thought I was alone in that dark place. But the two deep marks on the back of my hip would prove that to be a lie.

I wasn't alone in that place...and I'm not alone here either.

CHAPTER 1

IVY

It was the architecture that brought me to Edinburgh. I thought I could learn from the old buildings that have housed so many stories and all the places where so many lives have lived. The texture of the walls and the plants that have overgrown fallen castles. The romantic side of me was pulled to the fantasy of it all. My love of history is one thing, my desire for stories is another.

I thought my life in Scotland would be picturesque like the photos they show to prospective students to help them make their decision. My sabbatical only lasts so long and it's time for me to make a hard decision on what to do after my master's program is over. Real life as some would say, but I wasn't ready.

I'm not naive enough to believe that real life always turns out like a dream or a glossy photograph in a brochure.

I didn't expect everything to be so different. I could have never imagined what was to come. The unsettling feelings deep in the marrow of my bones. The chills that would come without warning. And yet...how it all would still call to me.

I pull my hood tighter over my head as I walk down the wet sidewalk. It's been raining most of the day. The pitter-patter and the harsh cold have been near constants. At first, they were soothing, nearly cleansing, but the gray skies have drained me almost as much as the nightmares have. I dare to peer up... The rain isn't quite rain right now. It's spitting, like it could become heavy fog any second.

The wind bites the tip of my nose. The rain is the kind that chills me to the bone.

The murky light reflects how I feel about this street and the sun, which is already mostly set. My boots click on the uneven stone walk as I pass the street as quickly as I can. Edinburgh looks older in the dark, as if the buildings are hiding secrets behind their doors and windows.

Some of those buildings *are* hiding secrets.

But I still find myself desperate to reach the café and go inside. The chill deepens despite the hood of my rain jacket, and I know it's *him*. Swallowing thickly, I quicken my pace.

He's stalking me. If he's even real... This city is making me think I'm losing my mind.

When I first came to Edinburgh, I thought I felt that way because I was alone in a new city without many friends. I've always been a loner, but I've never felt the loneliness that's haunted me here.

It was harder than I thought to find people to talk to. I had imagined forming a group of friends who would walk with me to the café and spread their notebooks and books out on the table with mine. I thought maybe we'd have so much to talk about that the barista might give us a look or two warning us to quiet down.

In my imagination, the barista would actually be fond of our meetings and might even sit down for tea or coffee with us, and we'd find out we had things in common and they would become part of our group.

I had so many fantasies of what these three months would become and not a damn one has come true.

The rain gets heavier as I reach the door of the café. The glass is clouded with the heat from the inside, and a quiet bell tinkles as I enter. Rain splashes as I take off my jacket and try to shake it over the threshold without letting any more rain in, but a spray of droplets falls to the floor.

I shoot an apologetic look at the barista, but she's looking down at something behind the counter and doesn't notice. It's a slight reprieve. Although the pit in my stomach has settled in with what feels like cement.

I take another peek over my shoulder as the warmth wraps around me and I realize she's new. I had at least learned the name of the young woman who's been here the majority of the time I've come: Tammy.

This woman though? I have no idea.

She's still looking down as I approach to order. For a few seconds, as I wait for my mug of hot water, I think about introducing myself to her.

That's probably asking too much of a barista. I come here because it's the place that's most familiar to me in Edinburgh, close to the lease I'm staying in, and maybe because I'm still holding out hope that I'll get a group of friends and I'll be able to say, *there's a place I always visit—it's small and cozy and I think you'd like it too.*

Maybe that would be a good time to introduce myself. I'm cold and my hair is damp, so I can't exactly put my best foot forward.

The steeps slowly rise in the mug, and I stand on the other side of the counter trying my best to warm up, but a chill runs over me.

The hairs on the back of my neck stand.

I close my eyes and breathe in the scent of coffee grounds and cinnamon. I can even smell the aroma of my tea starting to rise.

When I open my eyes, the barista is sliding the teacup across the counter to me on a coaster.

"Sugar is over on that table." The barista tilts her head to the side with a tight smile. "Enjoy."

I smile back at her although it wavers. She tells me the same phrase I hear every time I'm here.

With my hands mostly warmed, I doctor my tea with sugar and a little milk and take it to a table on the center wall.

I used to sit by the window, but a shiver deep in my spine warns me away.

It's him. The crazy thought seeps into my mind. My breath catches and I hope the barista doesn't see. It's all consuming.

The chill haunts me wherever I go. Even on

the rare sunny days, I feel it. I feel *him*. There have been days of this. Sleepless nights and long days of pretending I'm not crazy.

I wrap my hands around the cup of tea and try to convince myself I'm just overreacting.

My tote hangs heavier on my shoulder. The notebooks are there. Two of them. One for what I came for and the other for him. The sketches. The feelings. The nightmare that I'm terrified will return.

A shadow passes in front of the café window.

I can't help following it as it moves along. The shadow has a tall, wide shape of a person, but I can't see any features. The window is too fogged. The difference between the heat of the café and the cold of the rainy air outside is too great.

My heart pounds as the shadow slows down and pauses, like he can feel my eyes on him. Thump. Thump. My heart seems to slow, as does time.

I steal another glance at the barista. As quickly as I can, praying she sees it too. With one more thump of my heart I turn back, and he's gone, but the chill remains.

Another moment passes and it's then I realize my hands are shaking, my knuckles are white from gripping the mug so tightly. With effort, I relax my stance and tell myself it's nothing.

It's nothing but a nightmare.

These thoughts are only make-believe.

I sip my tea. It's still a bit too hot, burning my tongue mildly as it goes down, but the heat makes the chill a little less harsh. I focus on it. Focus on breathing deeply and grounding myself. Keep my feet here, in the present, in this moment.

A hot cup of tea, a quaint café, and a beautiful city filled with so much history.

Movement catches my eye and my entire body stiffens.

A couple of people walk by, just as blurry through the fogged-up window, moving fast.

It's nothing. There's nothing to worry about.

When I finally manage to relax into my chair, my face is hot. I fish my phone out of my pocket on instinct. I should call a friend just to hear another person's voice. Someone who could bring me back to reality.

But as I scroll through my contacts, another kind of chill sets in.

It had been hard to meet people when I first came here, but I had met a few people I've seen every so often and recognized.

I did have a group of friends back at home, but with the time difference and them moving and applying for jobs and internships and...moving on to the next phase, the messages have slowed.

Somehow, between now and the moment I set foot in this city, those people have faded out of my life. I've just felt so cold and isolated here. All the texts I've exchanged with people are from months ago. Those months flew by, despite the cold that seems to make every hour drag. It's been months, I realize. Months since I've had anything close to a social life.

Months I've spent alone under skies that always seem to be gray.

I hover over my friend Emily's name in my contacts list.

She'd answer, wouldn't she? I'm sure she'd accept an explanation about how I'd lost track of time studying and how I'd thought about texting her so many times and then got busy or tired, but now I could talk, and...did she want to?

With a reluctant breath, I put my phone away, snapping my jacket pocket shut over it.

I came here for hot tea on a rainy day and to do some studying, and that's what I'll do.

I get out one of my textbooks and the appropriate notebook. The words fade to gray and I find myself rereading the same paragraphs. I order another tea.

While it steeps, I clear my throat and introduce myself to the barista.

Her name is Cara, and she's taking a semester off. She doesn't say what she's studying, but she smiles when she talks about her routine, and I get through the conversation without bringing up the shadow outside the window or the chill I feel all over the city. I don't ask her if she's heard of anyone else experiencing anything similar. There's no way to slip a potential stalker into the conversation without freaking her out.

This time, when she pushes the fresh cup and saucer over to me, she says, "Enjoy, Ivy."

I thank her and take my tea back to the table.

Small steps. Progress. But it's quickly lost.

As soon as I sit down, I feel another chill.

I can't pretend I haven't felt it. I've been in the café long enough to warm up from the rain, and I haven't felt a draft. Nobody's even come in.

CHAPTER 2

CARLISLE

It's all gray and blurred. The darkness is everywhere and it moves about the unsuspecting people. And then there's her. Bright and so easily seen. She calls to me like I prayed to the gods she would. What I would give to be mortal again so she could see me as I see her.

Time...in time... I stop the thought, hating what must be done.

For now, my frustration only grows.

My focus drifts back to her in the present moment. The golden flecks in her deep brown eyes. Her long and lush dark brown hair. The soft curves of her face and the pale pink of her lips... breathtaking. She's gorgeous and her light shines wherever she goes. My eyes close and I swear I can still smell her. Her fragrance lingers in the rain.

I follow her—gorgeous curves, beautiful and sensual even under the fabric of her raincoat. I notice each shiver and the way she pulls her hood tight over her hair as if it will hide her from me.

Nothing could hide her from me.

Once she's gone into the café, letting out a gust of warm coffee-scented air into the cold, damp outdoors, and once the door is shut behind her, I stay out of sight and only watch. It's torture. Being so close, yet so far away.

She's only taking off her hood and sliding the raincoat off her shoulders, but even those simple movements heat my long-felt desire for her. The embers blaze deep in my soul. I watch as she runs her hand over her hair, combing her fingers through it and letting the droplets of rain disperse.

Every little thing she does is mesmerizing.

Heat courses through my body. I know her fear. It permeates around her, stifling what must be done. She's afraid of my presence because she doesn't know me, and that causes the deepest anger of all.

I don't mean to linger, but when I'm halfway

past, I realize I can see her.

The window is fogged with droplets running down the glass. In those thin tracks, I can see her face.

See her eyes. See them widen as she notices my presence. My heart rages with her. I can practically feel her blood pounding through her veins.

Recognize me, I plead silently. *Know me. You know me.*

But she doesn't. My throat tightens as I swallow, clenching and unclenching my fists. It's been too long and still I cannot contain myself.

For a minute I let myself imagine opening the door to the café. Would she run from me? If she saw me, would she sense fear or something else? If she truly *saw* me. Adrenaline courses through me and I debate what to do. She walks faster when she thinks I'm nearby. I can tell she's nervous by way she bites on her lip.

Part of me wouldn't mind a longer chase, but I'm past the point of wanting to drag this out. My heart beats impatiently. If there was a spark of recognition in her eyes, I might take the chance, but there isn't. There's only fear.

I've done terrible things in my existence. Horrid deeds. But nothing could prepare me for what I made a deal to do. With a steadying breath I tilt my head back, feeling the rain. Feeling alive in a way I haven't in so long.

I step away from the window and stay hidden behind the next building.

Waiting, planning, knowing I only have so much time.

When she comes out, she's already moving quickly. She pulls the hood of her coat over her hair and goes down the street almost at a run. Someone watching might think it's because of the rain. A damsel who does not care to be drenched.

But I know it's because she can sense me. I know it's fear that pushes her to move faster. Her fingers shake around her hood, and when it drops back off her hair, she doesn't try to pull it up again. She only runs faster, turning a corner up ahead and disappearing.

I'm so far away, and yet I swear I can hear her heart beat and her breath quicken.

I could follow her if I wanted, but I go the opposite direction instead. A deep sorrow clenches around every limb.

Another woman steps out of a building down the block. A woman I recognize and one who is very well aware of what's happening. I choose to follow her instead. A woman of influence and power. A beauty wars have been fought over.

Blonde hair, blue eyes, and fair skin. A Greek god who stands out in this muted world. She must be here for me. For us.

I quicken my pace and correct my features, heart pounding with very real frustration, but she makes it difficult, going faster, too.

I catch up with Aphrodite and fall into step at her side. Her light hair is swept back from her face, and she doesn't seem to care about the damp air.

"How long will it take?"

Her eyes flicker toward me. We've come to an intersection of two of Edinburgh's old streets. This woman isn't looking at me. She's only looking to see if there's traffic.

A car passes us, the tires squeaking on the cobblestones.

"How long will what take?" she asks.

I don't want to play these games. Getting straight to the point will be faster, although I pay my respects. She granted me this gift. It is only because of Aphrodite a demon can walk the realms of Earth. "How long will it take for her to remember?"

Aphrodite purses her lips. She glances into a dark storefront as we pass it. Nothing inside catches my eye, and nothing seems to catch hers, either. The street we're on and the storefronts seem meaningless.

All that matters is that Ivy remembers me.

"Those threads were cut," comes the reply. She's matter of fact. The goddess of love and beauty is short with me and my eyes widen, stinging with the past pain that clings to me harder the closer I get to her.

"But *I* remember." My heart thuds with the agony of remembering so much when the only love I've ever known remembers nothing. We've had lifetimes together. Every lifetime. My soulmate, my everything. Ripped apart only at our last death. The memories flash before my eyes. The rage and the brutal sadness.

"I've spent weeks following her around Edinburgh, hoping she'll turn around and her eyes will light up with all that's passed between us, but she's only getting further away. She walks fast on the street and ducks into cafés and shivers when she feels me following her like I'm a stranger who wants to do her harm."

Her pale blue eyes pierce into mine. "You weren't sent back. How can she remember what does not exist? How can she remember when the Fates cut the threads?" She is only factual. Logical. Although it feels cold, the gods have a way of coming off as such.

"She'll never remember?" I murmur the question, hoping for a different answer but knowing it won't come. Anger burns through me and a deep sadness that might even have echoes of fear swallows thickly at the idea that so many memories would be lost to her. Everything we shared, everything we built, everything we felt for one another can't be gone. I can't be the only one to carry those memories. The anger grows too intense for me to keep it under control, and I reach out in desperation for Aphrodite, pulling her to a stop on the sidewalk. "You told me she'd love me."

She blinks at my harsh whisper, her eyes sharp, then looks down at where my hand is wrapped around her arm.

"This isn't the underworld," she says, her voice scolding. My heart slows and I take a step back. The mere fact that Ivy will never remember begs a good part of my soul to be struck dead by her or any god.

"I was told a deal was made." I force myself to speak calmly, keeping my voice quiet so I don't attract any attention.

The woman sighs like I'm asking too much from her. I don't think I've asked enough.

"You never would've found her without me. You

wouldn't even be allowed to sneak into this realm. Remember that. None of this would have happened without my grace." Her eyes meet mine, and there's a dark judgment in them. "What you did…"

I glance down at the sidewalk for only a moment, pain clenching in my chest and heat burning in my face. These memories are just as painful as the idea of Ivy forgetting everything and never knowing me again.

"The threads being cut was a punishment I didn't deliver but one I understood. Know that."

With a tight throat I respond, "Hecate collects me for the army of the dead every night before the full moon under the last thread of light. I am doing what I can to make amends and repent."

I mean every word of it. I feel it all in the depths of my soul.

She speaks under her breath as the people walk by and we stand still. "You were meant to only feel betrayal and nothing more. Barely any time has passed and you still feel love for her…that is what convinced me. Do not disappoint."

I can only nod, swallowing thickly.

She looks away and begins walking again. I walk by her side, desperate to continue the conversation and at a loss for words. How I feel is mostly a howl of rage, and this woman will pretend not to understand.

"It would be wise of you to remember who I am and what I'm capable of," she warns.

"Yes, my lady," I answer diligently.

We pass several buildings. The mist is getting heavier. It'll rain again soon.

I think of her. And what tonight will be. Ivy stays inside when the sky opens up and the rain pours down. She'll shut herself in her room, wrap a blanket around her shoulders, and stay in until she has to leave again for a class or for her studies, and I'll spend every second fighting with myself.

Aphrodite goes into a hotel and passes the front desk without looking at the man behind it. He doesn't look up at us, either. We turn down a wide, dimly lit hallway with large sets of doors on either side. The lights flicker as she walks by.

As she's about to turn into an even darker hallway, she turns to face me, looking up into my eyes, and the shame I felt earlier comes back to me. I don't think it will ever let me go, but that's not what I need to know most of all.

"Is this more of a punishment, then?" It's difficult to force the words out, the question leaving my mouth in a rough demand. The goddess's lips press into a thin line. She has to know what this is doing to me. Maybe she even came here to taunt me with what she knows, and now she's glad to see that it's working. "To add on to my pain? To have her and for her not to know?"

I expect her to say yes. That would make the most sense, for this to be a cruel punishment I can't escape from.

She reaches out and touches my sleeve. I'm surprised at how soft the touch is.

"She will," she replies simply, and I let out a long breath. If this is out of pity or even a lie, I can't bring myself to accept that now. "She's going to love what you do to her," the woman continues, her tone almost wistful. But then her eyes harden again, and she looks at me with disapproval. "Perhaps you may act on such things before it's too late."

With the knowledge of what was suggested I do reiterated by yet another god, I stand numb, hating what must happen and yet hopeful.

She doesn't even look back at me. She just walks around the next corner and vanishes into a mirror.

CHAPTER 3

IVY

I can feel him watching.

The fluorescent lights of the grocery store seem to flicker, but I know it's not the wiring. It's been happening every time I've felt him. The texts I've read say when the lights flicker, there is someone with a message from the other side. Someone wanting to speak to you.

The goosebumps travel down my arms and back, causing my entire body to shudder. Somewhere deep inside, where intuition lies, tells me I'm not okay. It screams inside of me that my life is going to change forevermore. It's terrifying.

I swallow thickly, my heart pounds as if it's trying to escape. I glance around, but there's no one here. Just a narrow aisle next to another narrow aisle, and somewhere to the right I know there to be a cashier and a register. He's nowhere to be found at the moment though.

At that thought, I look up and at first, I think it's the man who's supposed to be at the register. My body freezes.

His face is etched as if carved from stone. Perfectly chiseled jaw, sharp piercing eyes. He's tall, his shoulders broad, he's beautiful in so many ways.

But instinctively I know. The air bows around him. Powerful. Deadly.

With careful steps, I pretend. I pretend I don't know deep in the marrow of my bones. I pray he can't see my hands tremble. I move to another aisle with my little wire basket hanging from my hand and he follows, too. Even my breathing is careful.

Every time I look over my shoulder to see if he's gone, he stares at the items on the shelves. As if he's not watching me. He hasn't done anything wrong. If I screamed, people would think I was paranoid.

But I know that the moment I look away, he goes back to watching me.

"I've had enough," I mumble under my breath,

feeling a lot less brave than I sound. I take a packet of tea bags off the shelf without looking to see what kind it is and stride up to the register to pay. I ring the bell as quickly as I can, and a woman comes out. Not the man who was here before.

My hands shake as I give my card to the woman behind the counter. If the woman behind the counter notices, she doesn't say anything. The small hairs at the back of my neck stand on edge as she scans the item and tosses it into a small brown paper bag.

I make a plan while she hands me my receipt. I'll leave the store and walk as fast as I can until I'm back in my room and lock the door behind me.

Once I've done that, I'll call every person I can think of and tell them what's been happening. If they think I'm crazy, I don't care. One of them will help me.

Even if I have gone mad here in this gray city.

I tuck the paper bag with my purchases into the crook of my elbow and head for the doors.

The man from the store comes after me.

I can feel his eyes the back of my neck, burning hot. He can't do this. He can't stalk me and stare at me and pretend he has any right to follow me all over the city.

I'm about to turn around and tell him so when I

feel it. A chill on the back of my neck and everywhere else. It's a warning. To run.

I clench my teeth and start walking. Fast, but not too fast. My heart pounds like I'm running. I wish I could run, but if I do, I know he'll run after me. He'll catch me so easily and there's no one here on the empty, narrow cobblestone street.

But there are people up ahead, coming in and out of shops and talking on their phones and looking up at the sky to see if the clouds are a different shade of gray today. As my heart races, they're almost all a blur. I walk too fast for how many people are on the sidewalk, but I don't care. My arm brushes against another woman's and I almost cry with relief. They're close enough to touch, and that means he can't do anything to me here. Not with so many people around.

I keep moving through the crowd, my bravery growing with every step. But he's behind me. He's right there behind me every time I look.

The chill bears down on me. I can almost feel him breathing on the back of my neck.

I whirl around, ready to scream for help, to tell him to get away from me and stay away from me, but nothing comes out of my mouth.

The strange man is gone. There's nobody behind

me. Nobody at all. The bustling sidewalks and streets are completely empty.

Where did they go? They were all just there.

Before I can scream, a hand comes from behind me and wraps around my throat.

I try to run, twisting away from his hand, but it doesn't work. I only make it a few steps before his hand is around my throat again, and his other hand is on my shoulder. The world becomes gray, all shades of it blurred.

He crowds me against a wall. Cold bricks press roughly into my back. My bag from the shop falls to the sidewalk. I hear it land with a crumpling sound, but I barely hear or see anything. All I can do is feel. He leans down over me, his body blocks the view of the empty street, and the darkness in his eyes terrifies me.

His hand comes back to my jaw, and I can't look away. Caught in his stare.

"You will come to me," he says. His voice is deep and almost seductive. So much different from what I imagined.

"No," I gasp, although it's so hard to breathe and even more difficult to stand. What happened to me? Tears prick as I murmur, "What have you done?"

His breath warms my neck and makes me shiver

more deeply than the chills that have followed me for months in Edinburgh.

My body falls heavy, as do my eyelids. I attempt to question, to accuse, but everything is weak.

"You aren't supposed to be here." After the words have warmed my skin, he presses his lips to the same spot. The kiss is soft but almost familiar. I tip my head against the bricks, sensation lighting me up all down my body.

The next gasp that escapes my lips is almost a moan. Confusion fills me, but it can't push out the tingling in my skin and the heat between my legs. I should be frozen with fear, but my body wants to arch into this demon's touch to get more of it. I'm shocked at myself. I'm shocked that this is how my body is reacting when my worst fears are coming true.

It must be a nightmare. None of this is real.

It doesn't feel real.

"Leave me alone." I barely manage, my words coming out as if slurred.

His eyes widen slightly, but then they narrow again, his dark gaze searing into mine.

"You will come with me," he repeats, slowly and clearly, stressing every word. My heart races even faster. "It is too dangerous for you here."

"No." I grit my teeth, refusing to let any tears escape though my eyes burn with more.

He looks into my eyes, then takes my wrist in his other hand. He lifts it into the light, turning it at different angles until the scar shows clearly and neither of us can ignore it.

"And what is this?" the demon asks, as if we're in a debate that he intends to win.

I jerk my wrist out of his grasp and press it tight to my chest, angling myself away from him.

"No." I back up a few steps. "That's none of your business, and I'm—"

"You already belong to me."

I open my mouth to say *no,* and my back hits a wall.

The wall shouldn't be there. Nothing comes from my lips but a gasp, and then I'm falling into the dark.

CHAPTER 4

CARLISLE

Nightshade kept her sleeping. Her falling prey to its venom was tortuous, and I don't care to think about what she's said nor what she's done without me beside her in this realm.

Holding her close to me is a balm to my pain.

I wonder if she sees terrors in her sleep that would compete with the nightmares that linger in the underworld. Her cream silk nightgown would cover her body in modesty, but I've draped a throw blanket from her sofa around her frame as one would a babe. Both to keep her warm in the depths of the underworld we must venture, and also to disguise her and keep what has happened from prying eyes as best I can.

A coil and a single strand of hair were required from each of us. I give them willingly as I've done so many times before. Past lifetimes and each time, I waited for her to meet Hermes and bring her to the river Styx. The memories flick through my mind as I hold her soft curves close, and Charon, the ferryman, takes us from the land of the dead to the river's bank.

The lights of the underworld, all the hells and heavens. With Hades' guard on my left and Asphodel Fields in front of me, I head toward the guard located just before the three judges, bypassing the field that makes you forget.

It was part of my punishment. I've done this so many times. But never with her in my arms.

My heart pounds as I make my way, my boots sinking into the soft ground, conscious of the eyes of judgement on me. It chills me to my core.

For thousands of lifetimes I've held Ivy in my arms, and for the first time it feels as though they'll take her away from me...again. In all black, dark eyes peer through the shadow of the cape that drapes over the guard's head. I've never seen his face. But I know the guard that waits for Lord Hades' men.

Screams of terror are vaguely heard in the distance. This is the marketplace of souls. Where mortals are tested, where the weight of their morality is judged, possibly, for all eternity.

I start, clearing my tight throat, "I am of the army of the dead and—"

"You may pass," he says beneath his breath, barely sparing a glance.

My shoulders rise with a desperate need to move. To obey before he changes his mind.

"My thanks to Lord Hades," I state, bowing my head and rushing toward my chambers with her in my arms. Her head lulls from side to side and I know she'll wake soon.

The locking of the stone door with the iron key is harsh and loud. The "thunk" echoes in my chambers and that's what wakes her.

She gasps as I lay her down in a high-ceilinged room with dark walls and thick pillars, everything expertly crafted to keep the space and balance and give a sense of awe to anyone who enters. Ivy seems both awed and terrified as reality dawns on her.

The beauty of her serene expression at peace

in my arms vanishes and with her widened darting eyes comes the pain of her not knowing.

Ivy glances around, taking it in.

Her new home. *Our* new home.

Her body is stiff as if a prey realizing it's been caught in a trap. Her beautiful gaze lands on the furnishings, each piece dark and solid, yet welcoming. The side tables and rugs are a mix of antiques fit for a palace, the richness in the curved wood and polished shine that never gets dull. Artwork painted by the most skilled hands in the underworld hangs on the walls. Every piece I picked with her in mind. Little memories of her in each piece. It was Hades' version of hell I was destined to live. He said it was a gift. A compromise that was fair and just. And for so long I've lived without the one thing that gives me peace.

When he offered me this chance to have her, there was no reality in which I would refuse his deal.

Her eyes skip over the pieces. I can tell she wants to linger on some of them, but she doesn't. Ivy's only glancing at the elegance surrounding her. Even now, she frantically searches for a way out.

There is only one door. And with a flick of my wrist, the magic of this realm takes the key away.

As she scrambles for an exit, on shaky limbs, I

can only look at her.

Her full lips. Her doe eyes. The fear in her expression, but also a desire that's so close to the surface I can't ignore it.

I don't care if this is meant to be a punishment or a test. I'm too consumed with Ivy's closeness.

I stalk toward her, slowly, and she freezes, her gaze focuses on me. Her eyes widen. She understands that for now she's my prey, and I'm going to have her.

I'm impatient for her. More impatient than Ivy can ever know. I want her curves under my hands. Her warmth pressed against me. I crave her and for her to remember. I wish to tilt her face to mine so I can capture her mouth. I even desire her defiance. That spark she has reminds me of everything we'll have again.

Ivy backs up one more step and her back hits the windowsill. She grasps for it without turning, her hands finding the edge, and lets out a small sound at her discovery that there's nowhere else to run.

The iron press around my heart is turned tighter. The fucking pain I feel staring at her with such fear in her eyes is unbearable. Nearly so. Not nearly what it was when they told me she would be lost to me forever.

She has to look, then, turning her head to see

out large windows behind her. Ivy must know from the inside of the tower that this place is like a castle. Not unlike the old city I tore her from. Not all of the underworld is this. The view outside should only confirm it.

"There's nowhere else," I tell her with a touch of a sympathetic tone, in case she's still thinking there's a means of escape she hasn't found yet. "You might find joy in the view I offer here." She does not know, but a lifetime ago—a few of them—we lived in Edinburgh. They gifted me this home because of that. A blessing and a curse.

"Take me back," she demands.

"There is no way to do that," I tell her honestly. "Not until the gods allow. Here is where we will remain forevermore."

Ivy jerks her head around, eyes blazing. "This is—"

"This isn't real," she says, almost to herself. "None of this is real."

"If it's not real, then let me enjoy you," I offer. Desperate to kiss her. Desperate for her to stop fighting and fearing me.

She pauses, her chest rising and falling as she calms right before me. Her eyes drift down my body and then back to my stare. *Please. Let me help you remember.*

"Enjoy?" She plays as if she doesn't know what I'm suggesting.

"Touch you," I say, taking a step forward. "Kiss you," I add. My feet stay planted though, not wanting to push her too much too quickly. "If it's not real, there should be no harm."

Ivy only leans against the sill, her heart racing fast enough for me to hear it pound and see her pulse fluttering in her neck. I breathe in deep, getting as much of her scent into my lungs as I can. It's been weeks of following her through that rainy city, with storms that constantly try to wash her away, and I won't take this closeness for granted.

"I promise you'll enjoy it, too." She will. I wouldn't do anything less for her. She doesn't have to believe me now, but I'll show her.

"Do I know you?" she finally asks in a murmur.

"Yes," I answer, hope cracking that vice.

"What do you want with me?" she asks.

"To love you."

"This isn't real," she whispers again. When she smiles, the muscles in her throat tighten and my gaze is drawn there, my desire to kiss her just behind the shell of her ear intensifies. *She loves it when I do that.*

I move across the floor to her, closing the distance between us. Ivy stiffens at the windowsill, but there is truly nowhere else to go—she can only lean as far as the glass, and she's not even doing that. I knew it. I knew part of her remembered me. Part of her craves my touch the way I have been craving hers. Her fast breaths tell me how much she's wanted this and how she told herself she was afraid.

She can be afraid, if that's how she feels, but she won't be afraid for long. She'll feel so much more than fear now that I have her with me.

So much more.

I lower my lips to her neck, bending slowly and deliberately, and at the last second, Ivy lifts her chin and gives me more access to her tender skin.

She gasps when my lips touch her neck, her heart beating hard just underneath her skin, and I groan into her heat when her back arches toward me.

My heart pounds with hot blood and desire like I've never known.

My Ivy.

"Ivy," I murmur with devotion.

She makes a needy sound in the back of her throat and presses closer. Every inch of my skin remembers her touch. My entire body feels the need to hold her, to love her, to be enveloped in her scent.

I can feel how conflicted she is and at the same time how relieved she must be. This is not the touch of a woman who considers me a stranger. "Give in to me," I whisper as if it's a demand, but instead it's a plea.

Ivy throws her arms around my neck and pulls herself in closer, her breath warm on my cheek. It's fucking heaven. *She's* my heaven.

I drag my lips up her neck until I capture her sweet mouth. And then I lick into her, tasting her deeply. Her body is warm and soft under my hands, and her arms flex around my neck as I run my palms over her curves. I remember every bit of her body.

She makes soft noises into the kiss that don't sound like protests at all.

I know that she likes it when I run the pad of my thumb under her breast and tease at one of her nipples. She likes it when I pull her in by the waist so she can feel how hard I am under my clothes. She likes it when I slip my hands under her clothes and take them off one by one, like I'm unwrapping her. Like she's a precious gift, which she is, even if she's being used to torment me, even if she's being tormented herself for no reason I can fathom.

I expose her curves to the light of the underworld, lifting her nightgown up, and dip my head to kiss her collarbone.

Ivy throws her head back and lets her eyes flutter closed, clearly relishing the sensation, even if she's too afraid to watch me give it to her.

It doesn't matter if she can't look at me yet. I don't care. If she concentrates on feeling, she'll remember. Every touch will help her remember. I have to keep my mind on that goal—every touch will bring the Ivy I know closer to the surface.

Even if it doesn't, I'm too swept up in her to stop. The ache in my cock spreads until it's everywhere in my body. My arms flex. I lick up the line of her neck, then over her other nipple, drawing a soft moan from her lips, then get to my knees and spread her thighs.

Ivy balances precariously on the sill while I open her to me and push my face into the soft, wet folds that I've been missing like I would miss my own heart.

She cries out, sweet and low, when I lap my tongue over her clit, gasping with every flick against the sensitive nerves. The soft *oh*s she lets out are pleas for more, though Ivy won't let herself say the words. Either she doesn't know my name or she won't allow herself to say it.

I'll make her say it. I'll make her remember that she knows my name, that she knows me. She already knows she wa_

she *needs* this.

Ivy arches her back ag_

firmly into my face.

I drink her in like I'll ne_

Ivy cries out, coming c_

first of many orgasms I'll gi_ ___ orgasms,

if she wants them, and the taste of her sweetness

overwhelms me.

I have to have her stretched out under me, so I

lift her from the sill and capture her mouth again

while I take us to the wide, cream, velvet chaise that

she'd looked at before. Ivy sighs when I lay her out

on it, a noise that hitches as if she's giving in.

I can hardly spare the time to strip myself of my

clothes. I shove at them carelessly until more of me

is exposed.

That's when Ivy reaches for me. It's the first

time she's done it deliberately, her eyes hot as she

drags her fingertips down the front of my chest. My

cock twitches from that touch alone. Her eyelashes

flutter in lust. And she drags her fingertips down the

front of my chest. I love it. She feels like heaven.

"Please," she says under her breath, as if she can't

bear to say it any louder. "Please."

There's no reply I can make to communicate how

urgently I need

her legs a_

cock. _

a_

her, so I simply slot myself between nudge her opening with the head of my she buries her head in the crook of my neck kisses me. My Ivy kisses me in the tender spot as her legs wrap around my hips. My heaven. My Ivy. My heaven.

Ivy gasps as I push in, then gasps again, the sound becoming a quiet moan as I fill her completely.

I close my eyes, relishing the sensation. I've needed this so much.

I've needed to feel her more than I needed my own sanity.

I'm gentle at first but with a single moan of "more," I allow myself to fuck her more ruthlessly. Rutting into her and loving the pleasure and lust that covers us in the heat of the moment. Everything I remember, and more, because we've been separated.

Her moans are exactly the same. Her voice breaks and rises exactly the same. I haven't lost her.

She comes on my cock as I drive into her, fucking her mercilessly, just the way she likes. Ivy clings to me, throwing her head back, dragging her wet mouth over my skin, biting wherever she can sink her teeth into my skin.

I can feel her everywhere around me, that sweet, tight sense of home.

"Ivy," I growl into her neck, unable to stop myself, unable to hold back. It's the only word that means anything to me. "My heaven."

CHAPTER 5

IVY

I don't know what came over me. As I lie alone in the bed, with satin sheets and lush pillows, I stare at each brick on the wall wondering where the hell I am. I've never seen such a place. Not in all my life, in any text...except for those of fantasies.

What happened? Where am I? And why can't I wake up?

I never should have acted like that. I never should have touched him like I wanted him. I shouldn't have looked at him like he could ever be anything to me other than the man who stole me off the street.

There is no pain and hardly any fear here, and I

don't understand.

The man who followed me around Edinburgh. The man who said I wasn't safe in the city, then stole me away and brought me here, only to keep me in the same room, never allowing me to leave... I kissed him. And I loved it. Something inside of me stirred in a way I can't understand or justify.

Questions race in my mind and all the while I stare at the luxury around me wondering what drug I've taken.

The sheets are the softest I've ever felt. The pillows are filled with down, firm but plush at the same time. Even the sheets and blankets that cover me to the waist feel silky, far nicer than any blankets I've ever had on my own bed. If I went back to my room now, I'd probably be surprised at how rough those sheets are in comparison.

But they would be my sheets, and it would be my bed, not this stranger's in this odd place that doesn't feel real.

I roll over to face the window and sigh.

It can't be real, can it? This whole place, and the world outside, can't be real. And yet I touch my chest and can feel my heartbeat. I pinch my skin and feel the sharp pain, and yet I do not wake.

Because the world outside looks like something

out of a story. A fairy princess type of story, where a girl is taken out of her life and brought to a magical land, or at least a land she's never seen before. It's like something preserved from the past, but not the past of any city I've visited. It's different, and I don't recognize it. The tower of the castle we're in must be high because for as far as the eye can see, I see lights and cities. The bright white gates and pillars of onyx and amethyst. Roads of gold and pristine pyrite. It's all unreal. A mist and smog of fire covers a place in the distance, and I vaguely remember myths of the underworld.

I slide my hand under the cool pillow and let my eyes blur the world outside. There's no point in looking. I can't get out. The door to this room is locked. I've tried it three times, and it never opens.

I should say—it *only* opens when he comes in. It's like he's read my mind, because the door swings open almost silently as I think of him. I hear the *whoosh* as he steps inside because there's no other sound in this place.

Chills run over my skin like they did before, and yet it's different. It's nearly like foreplay. What has he done to me?

"My heaven," he murmurs and then says my name clearly. "Ivy?" I pick myself up, pulling the sheet with me to cover myself and meet his eyes.

He appears in my line of sight with something in his hand.

A necklace.

I still feel naked when he looks at me, his eyes slipping from my face to the curves of my body, and I look back at him, pretending my heart isn't racing.

With the necklace in one hand, he offers the other to me.

I resist a moment, a blush rising to my cheeks. "I'm not decent."

Without a word he opens a cupboard and my jaw nearly drops, it's filled with beautiful dresses. Simple and floor length, almost like nightgowns but far too luxurious. He chooses one and again without a word he helps me slip it on. It fits perfectly, hugging my waist and hanging so beautifully. The deep burgundy is beautiful against my pale skin.

"Now?" he questions and holds out his hand again.

I take it and let him help me out of the bed. No point in fighting.

"Where are we going?"

He doesn't answer. He just leads me across the room to a large, ornate mirror leaning on the opposite wall. The mirror is so tall that he can see all of himself in it.

I look small next to him. This beast of a man. He's beautiful. His eyes especially. They say you can see someone's soul in their eyes and I swear I can in his. And when I look at him, tears prick my eyes although I don't know why.

I rip my gaze away before the feeling turns too heavy.

He positions me in front of him and places the necklace around my neck, letting the jewel at its center settle into the dip in my throat. His eyes rake over me in the mirror while his fingers work carefully at the clasp, trailing over my dress like he can see underneath it.

"This will stay on you always," he says, his voice low and commanding. "So they know."

"So *who* knows?" I wish his voice didn't have any effect on me.

"And," he continues, as if I haven't spoken, "I'll always know where you are."

"It will track me?" I question, hating the idea and feeling more like a prisoner.

"This is a large place, and I don't want to worry."

"I'll be allowed outside?" I ask and he smirks, a huff of a laugh leaving him.

"A bit excited, are you?" he asks just beneath his

breath before brushing my hair off my shoulder and kissing my skin in the crook of my neck. Against my conscious will, a moan slips from me and my eyes close.

When I open them, his eyes meet mine in the mirror "So long as you have this on, you will be safe and if you are lost, they will be able to help you get back home."

He touches the jewel in the center, circling it with his fingertip. My nipples harden thinking of his touch.

"Who is *they*?" I ask, meeting his eyes in the mirror.

He drops his hand away from the necklace, bringing his grip to my waist. Possessively. And it makes no sense at all that I would love it as I do.

"That's none of your concern for the moment." He straightens behind me, staying close enough for me to feel the heat of his body. "Now that you've taken what you wanted, you can…"

My hand flies to the necklace. "*You* gave this to me. I took nothing."

He smirks at me in the mirror as if I've said something amusing, but the delight on his face doesn't last. His face darkens, and he leans down to drag the tip of his nose along my neck.

Goosebumps race down my body. I want him *so* badly, and it's like being lit on fire. These touches are hardly anything, but I'm hot under my dress.

I inhale more heat and more conflicted emotion, too. I shouldn't want this man at all. I can only justify it by convincing myself that none of this is real. It's certainly not a reality I've ever lived before.

His lips brush my jaw and he groans roughly. "I need you again."

The sound that comes out of my mouth is almost a moan. I meant to say *no*, but the truth is that I want him to touch me. I want him to take me.

So I press myself harder against him and lift my dress to my hips, bunching the fabric in my fingers. I give in to the idea of pleasure with him. To the thought of seeing more of this place. And more of him.

His hands roam over my thighs, and I use one hand to keep my dress in front of me so I can balance on the mirror.

It's a sight like none other to watch his large hands skim over my skin, touching me like I'm delicate and irreplaceable. His hands skim lightly over my hip bones and down to my thighs. I spread my legs for him the moment he touches me there.

It's shameful, but I want his fingers on my clit

again. He knew just how to play me. Another moan escapes me as he circles, gathering heat between my legs.

"That's it," he says in my ear. "Aren't you beautiful? Gorgeous. I could look at you forever."

The sensations he brings alive in me are too intoxicating to ignore. I have to have more of them. He's addictive.

The slightest added pressure on my clit makes me melt against him. Makes me spread my thighs wider and moan. I lean my head against his shoulder, needing the contact.

Fuck, what does this man have over me?

He grips my hip and encourages me to bend backward until he can grind against my naked skin. The fabric covering his cock meeting my most sensitive parts steals my breath. He's hard underneath his clothes.

Wanting me. He acts as if he's desperate for me. I've never felt so pulled to another person before. So desired.

I desire him just the same.

He plays me like a well-used toy, stroking my nipples, plucking at them until I let out a whine. Then he kisses my earlobe.

"There is magic here," he says, his voice husky

and rough as if he'd spent hours thinking about me. "I can give you pleasure like you've never known."

I keep my eyes closed, barely hearing him. Magic. This place is magic. And he's a magician of pleasure.

He brings the pad of his thumb back to my nipple and teases it until it's full and hard. I'm so desperate for sensation that I arch against him, rolling my hips as he strokes my clit.

I close my eyes and give in to it. Why does it have to be so good? Why does it have to take over every part of me? It makes me lightheaded. It almost makes me forget where I am and how I got here.

"Will you let me go?" I gasp.

He goes still, his fingers hovering over my clit. When I open my eyes, he's looking into mine in the mirror, his eyes dark.

"You already know." His tone isn't as demanding as I anticipated, more sympathetic than anything. Before I can respond he kisses me, and it's just like forgetting. Like silencing thoughts that feel like they don't belong here anymore.

He moves his fingers again, sending pleasure through my core, and nudges his cock between my legs. He keeps playing with my clit as he sinks into me inch by inch. I spread my legs to give him more room, although something in me says I don't need to. He'll move me the way he wants.

I drop my dress so I can brace myself on the mirror. My body rocks with his hips, moving back and forth as he thrusts in and bottoms out and strokes again. My thighs tremble. Our reflection a sinful decadence that stares back at me every time I dare to open my eyes.

"I *don't*," I manage to reply. It's hard to get words out when all my body wants to concentrate on is him.

"You were mine in a previous life." My gaze meets his in the reflection and my heart hammers.

Still buried in me, he reaches for a box behind the mirror. Old, wooden, and carved.

At first I pull back, uncertain, but he kisses my neck. "It's for you," he murmurs. With one hand caressing my body, his lips leave kisses in a trail down my neck while his other hand opens the box.

Inside is a small iron dish, two tall spindle candles, one black and one white twined together and bathed in what looks like herbs of jasmine and what smells like clove. A few small crystals, rose quartz, and the box is filled with rose petals that have long dried.

"You were mine in a previous life," he repeats, "and I want you to remember."

His eyes stay on mine in the mirror. Nothing

in his expression says that he's lying. He believes it's true.

He looks at himself, then a spark is in his eyes that should be familiar. I should know where I've seen it before, but when I try to search my memory, there's nothing there.

"I don't remember that," I say. "I don't remember anything."

Why do I wish I remembered?

"Light it with me," he murmurs, and with both of his hands he stands the candles on the plate, placing the items around them, and lights a match. With the flame, he ignites the black candle and then hands me the match.

With my back to his chest and his cock still inside of me, I take the match and without thinking, I do it. I light the white candle and barely get to blow the match out before he devours me.

"I'll help you remember." His voice breaks as he thrusts in deep, pulling a gasp out of me as well. He fucks me like a savage, rough and raw. I cry out and my hands fall forward onto the mirror. The flames lick and burn to the right of the mirror.

His arm comes between my breasts, bracing me to him as he fucks me. Pulling pleasure from deep within me. We're locked together in the mirror, my breath beginning to fog the glass as we come together. Pleasure ignites from deep in my core.

He doesn't stop and I can barely take any more. From the corner of my eyes, I barely get a glimpse of the candles as they light on fire, burning to nothing more than a pool of wax that covers the rocks and petals on the plate. The deed is done so quickly it cannot be taken back.

He drops his lips onto my shoulder and with a low grunt, spills the last of his release, his arms locking tight around me.

He pulls out slowly, like he doesn't want to, then lets my dress fall back to the floor. It only takes a few seconds for him to put himself back together, straightening his clothes and tucking himself away. All the while I'm breathless and ravaged, barely able to sit upright.

CHAPTER 6

CARLISLE

I don't want to tell her my name. For so many years I've dreamed of her remembering. If the spell cast doesn't work... I begin to fear and then take it back. Doubt is the killer of magic.

It's late when I enter the room and I can barely breathe. All is dark outside the window and the sconces are dimmed to a level that won't disturb anyone who is asleep.

Ivy's asleep. I know it when I step through the door, and not just because of the lights.

I close the door behind me and cross the room with careful footsteps.

Alone in the bed, curled under the covers, she's small and delicate. If she could see herself, I know she'd wish she didn't look so vulnerable, pulling the blankets tight over her shoulders. She is though and she always has been.

I saw it in her eyes in the mirror—how much she wants to take from me, how much she wants to ask of me, how she searches my face for any hint of her memories and finds nothing.

It must feel like a betrayal, her body responding to mine so intensely. My desire for her is undeniable. She is my home and my heaven, and all I wish is for her to remember my name. Remember how much I love her and how much she loved me.

I felt her shake out small orgasms and high peaks all over me. I think they'd have gone on forever if I gave her more pleasure. Her body lifted toward mine every time I touched her skin. Ivy arched back for me, reaching, trying to get more contact.

The memories of only a single moment are enough to fill the deepest pits of despair in my heart. The places left empty and cold when they tore her from me.

I don't care what threads have been cut, new threads can be stronger. They will be. I know it.

And I can never deny her. I can only show her as

much of the truth as I have.

The fireplace in the corner of the room cracks and cackles with the flames licking along the never-ending fire. It's as if a confirmation of my thoughts.

I hope that part of her feels it. Part of her must remember how it was before, because she's burned into my soul. How could I not be part of hers?

Carefully, and with a small creak of the mattress, I sit on the edge of the bed and watch her breathe. Her face is soft and relaxed in sleep. The last time I saw her like this was before I left—before the war, before I killed and was killed myself.

That was centuries ago. All those years weigh on my mind, crawling by like an eternity, each one lasting a thousand years. Every hour I spent apart from her stretched out until I thought I'd snap from the weight.

I fought for the wrong side and paid the consequences. But I was a warrior they wanted to keep, a weapon they wanted to wield. I'm grateful I do not burn in the pits of fire along with the Titans, but my hell was one and the same without her.

But now she's here, and those centuries seem like a moment.

I crave to touch her so badly, to prove to myself she is real, that my palms ache, but I settle for placing my hand close to hers on the bed.

Now that she's in the underworld and in my bed, though, there's another problem.

Hecate comes for the army of the dead at the last sliver of light from the waning moon this evening. I must fight and lead her armies.

Tonight, fear weighs heavily on my chest, making it hard to breathe. My mouth is dry from thinking about leaving Ivy. It's the kind of fear I haven't felt so intensely since Ivy and I were separated, but now it's as if it never left me.

I fear they will take her from me again. My gaze lingers on her necklace. She assured me she will be safe. Hades and Aphrodite both. And yet...

If the gods know of one emotion it is the joy they receive from testing mortals.

There are sounds in the distance, almost too quiet to hear through the thick walls of the tower and the glass meant to shelter the interior from those noises. I hear the barking in the distance anyway. One glance out the window, and I can see the torches lighting the way. The army is gathering.

With a slow exhale and a gathering of strength, I turn my attention back to Ivy, resting peacefully and without a worry of the judgment that will be brought down in the mortal realm tonight.

I let myself stay on the bed for a few more minutes, closer to her warmth.

I close my eyes and listen to Ivy breathing. What is she dreaming about? Does she dream about me?

I would give anything to lie down beside her and join her in those dreams.

But I cannot do that. Not tonight.

As I move through the preparations, the fear in my chest grows. I clench my teeth against it. A small voice inside me begs to stay with her.

I *should* stay with her. I've brought her here, and walking away again might keep us apart for centuries more.

I stand in front of the fireplace and watch the flames in the grate, my emotions already battling inside me. Should I wake her? Should I put my hand on her shoulder and coax her into consciousness just so I can hear her voice? So I can tell her I will not be back tonight, not until the new moon has blackened the sky.

My stomach clenches as the fire burns brighter. It's as if the flames have leaped out of the grate and settled in my gut. It's a feeling of pure dread, and my heart beats with uncertainty.

How can I leave her here?

The more important question is, how can I stay?

I must complete my duty. It is my purpose as much as it is my punishment.

I steal another glance at her. All of my tortured thoughts haven't woken her.

I take a final breath. Before I can exhale, a hand comes down on my shoulder.

I open my eyes and turn to find Hades standing there—tall, dark haired, fiercely foreboding. A shiver goes down my spine. Although I've seen him many times and know him as well as I could hope to, being in his presence always makes me feel this way. I imagine I will always feel terror in his presence. For he alone casts the final judgment. Your heaven or hell for eternity is but for his design. That kind of power over one's soul is far more than daunting.

I swallow against my dry mouth and nod in greeting, unable to speak. He seems to sense that I can't get any words out, because he returns my nod and drops his hand to his side.

Finally, I manage to bow my head, "My lord," I greet him. "I did not hear you enter." The cold shadow of power that surrounds him envelopes my very being. His very presence evokes fear. Hades, lord of the underworld and king of the dead. He does as he wills and so it will be for all souls.

In this moment though, I feel calm with the

manner in which he looks down at me. In the centuries I have served him, I have known him to be just and fair, even if that requires harshness and brutality. His decisions are swift and heavy. My heart races feeling his presence. Before fear can linger, he speaks.

"You will stay tonight," he says evenly, his voice deep and gravelly. He glances at Ivy, who sleeps quietly, unbeknownst to her that the king of the underworld stands at the foot of her bed. "You have business here and you have served me well."

Shock and gratitude rock through me. My eyes widen as I stare up at him in disbelief.

"My lord?" My heart beats faster, harder. I don't dare to hope, but I've spent centuries living on hope. On the smallest chance that I would have Ivy again to hold and cherish.

"I will need you for business as well...shortly," he states and I eagerly agree to whatever it is that he may require of me.

"Hecate—" I begin. I can't simply stay here. That's never been a choice.

"I have told her," Hades says.

The fire in my chest burns brighter than ever. It burns brighter than I thought it ever could again. The sweet relief of being granted permission to stay could take me to my knees if I let it.

"I..." There are no words that will allow me to thank Hades the way he should be thanked. Not for this. He's handed me my life back. "Thank you, my lord."

"Stay with your soulmate," he says with finality. This is an order I don't intend to refuse. I'll never leave her again. "She may not remember," he says, "but I do and I come with a gift. Remember this when I need you once again."

"Hades, my lord..." At a loss for words, I accept the box but Hades doesn't release it at first. With the heavy iron box between us he says, his dark eyes piercing mine, "You doubt your power but you do not dare to doubt mine. I give her back to you, and in return you will aid me."

I nod, wordlessly, and he nods in return before leaving me in silence and with the contents of the iron box.

CHAPTER 7

IVY

I wake up suddenly to a pressure at the end of the bed. My body is tight at first, startled and still. But then I remember.

It's him. It's odd as the room focuses before my blurred vision, I don't seem to crave what once was. It's warm and comfortable and there's something here that begs me to find it. I can feel it. It's like a whisper I can't quite make out.

I blink, bleary-eyed, and sit up, rubbing at my eyes.

It's been a long time since I fell asleep. I feel rested and also think that it must be the middle of the night, if things like the middle of the night even exist in this place. Whatever time it is, it's late, and everything is dark outside the window.

He holds out his hand to me.

Am I getting used to him? Am I getting complacent? Or is there truly magic in this place? Because something so unsettled inside of me feels at peace when I look into his eyes.

What's the right thing to do if you might be stuck somewhere forever? With every minute that goes by, I believe him a little more.

If he says forever, I'll be here forever.

And I don't want to admit it, but I wonder what that would be like. Forever. That's more than one lifetime.

His words chased me in my sleep, telling me we've loved each other for lifetimes before.

Hesitantly, I put my hand in his. Our fingers slide together like we were meant to hold one another, and my heart twists again, wanting more of his comfort.

"What is it?" I ask. "Is something wrong?"

"Come see what I've done."

I'm not sure what I'm seeing at first, and then my eyes adjust to the low light and the brighter lights within.

There are red candles, thin and tapered and lovely, on a gold tray. This isn't decorative. The candles have been burned before, as part of a ritual that someone took great care with. Something about the tray tells me that it's important.

Rose petals surround the candles. This time freshly picked, and their scent carries through the room. A shell on the right side is filled with water and crystals, shining beneath the surface: pink and black and clear. There is a mirror behind it, reflecting the low light in the room and a glass decanter filled with dark red wine. The candle flames dance in the mirror, and that tiny voice says *you should recognize this.*

It feels like something I've known forever and yet I do not understand.

All I recognize is how his hand tightens on mine.

"Sit," he says, and helps me lower myself to the floor, swallowing thickly. It's warm, which I didn't expect—almost as warm as the bed and comfortable to sit on. Is he doing that, or is the hard stone making itself better for me? Maybe I'm not as rested as I thought.

My breath comes quicker as I look over the tray from this distance. The gold gleams in the candlelight, and I know how those candles would feel if I reached out to touch the warm wax with the droplets running down the tapers.

I don't. I fold my hands in my lap, sitting cross-legged with him beside me, and watch as he lifts the cup from the tray and offers it to me.

"Drink," he says, the candlelight flickering in his eyes, "and you'll remember."

"What will I remember?" I dare to ask him and then stare up into his eyes. The light from the fire in the corner of the room dances in his dark eyes.

"That our love was a gift from the gods. One they could take away," he says and then lifts the goblet, "and one they can give back."

I trust him. Perhaps I am a fool. But I've never wanted the sweetness of wine so much in my life as I do when he offers it to me. I tell myself again, it's all a dream anyway. And if none of this is real, if the consequence has no bearing, why should I not give in to my heart's desires.

I take the glass. It's heavier than I expected, and I have to hold it with both hands.

The wine is a deep, rich color and I inhale its scent. It smells dry and slightly flowery, and once again excitement makes my heart beat a little faster.

He leans over the cup and kisses me. The heat of his lips on mine steadies me. Tension goes out of my shoulders and my back. He's a soothing balm. The power he has over me is uncanny.

He breaks the kiss softly, then takes my chin in his hand and turns my head toward the mirror. My hair is a messy halo and my eyes are tired, but together, the two of us, there is beauty.

"Watch the flames," he says, and just like that, it's all I can focus on. Those flames twisting in the mirror, multiplying until there are endless copies in the glass.

I watch, letting my eyes roam over them one by one.

He maneuvers himself behind me and lowers his head to kiss that spot on my neck. It must be his favorite spot on my body, he's always kissing me there. More shivers move down my spine. Shivers of pleasure and desire and a deep longing.

Slowly, so I don't spill any of the wine, I lift the cup to my lips, keeping my eyes on the flames, and tip it up until the wine meets my lips.

The full-bodied flavor of the wine bursts on my tongue.

I take another sip, and his lips meet my shoulder again, lingering there, pressing warmth into my skin. His hand is on my waist, holding me upright. I know I won't fall backward. I won't fall anywhere with him wrapped around me.

Something about the wine calls to me. I've tasted the flavor before. I *know* I have. If I just taste a little more, I'd know where I drank it, and who I was with, and—

I want to close my eyes and lean my head against his shoulder, but I don't. The lick of the flame in the mirror begs me to watch, but it blurs even as I blink and try to keep my eyes focused on it. Is the mirror blurring or is the world blurring? Or is it only my eyes?

Another kiss to the side of my neck sends heat rushing through my body. Heat and possession and something else.

Hope?

The mirror continues to blur, but the flame remains strong, burning brighter, almost as if it's trying to keep my attention.

I let out a moan, and then I hear myself, as if from a great distance, moan again.

Chills flow over my skin. The world seems to shake and blur.

I have a flash of him, close to me, on top of me. Him taking me from behind, seated. The length of his body warm underneath mine. My body working against his in a steady rhythm.

It's as vivid as a photograph. All of the times he's kissed me. In a field with the wind in my hair, on the stone steps of a cottage, while I'm crying, young and naive, and lying in bed when he brushes my hair—hair that has turned gray—from my face. They all flicker before me and tears brim.

Memories flash through my head. I can feel his hands on every inch of my body, feel the way he's touched me—not just once, but hundreds or thousands of times.

The murmurs of him loving me. And I say it back.

Tears fall and he brushes them away.

It cannot be real, I tell myself. But everything feels as if it's happened over and over again.

The memories come in short flashes of him taking me, filling me, stretching me around him, heightening my pleasure and pushing me higher and higher and higher until I tumble off the peak.

I remember the pleasure nearly blinding me as he filled me again, on another day, on another night, tangled in another set of sheets and blankets. I see the light on his face from the sun and the moon and from the morning to the evening. I see him lying next to me on the bed, limp and sated, the sweat on his body slowly cooling as a warm breeze blows over us.

"I'll love you forever, Ivy," he tells me.

And I murmur his name. I promise to love him. I see our first kisses and our lasts.

There are so many flashes. I feel like I could drown in them. I want to run my fingers through them. I want to stay in one for longer than a heartbeat.

And then, suddenly, there's no more wine and all that exists is him behind me in this very room and the tears that have settled just on my upper lip. The cup is empty, and it weighs heavily in my hands.

He leans down in front of me and blows out the candles. The darkness is abrupt, but I don't have the energy to gasp.

I'm shaken from what I've just seen and felt and known to have been.

"Come with me," he commands as he stands in the quiet room.

I don't think I can stand, but he helps me to my feet and guides me back across the room. My knees feel weak as I fall into the mattress, grateful for how soft it is as it cradles me.

He pulls the blankets over me and looks into my eyes.

"You will find your place here," he says. "You will."

"What is your name?"

I try to remember. I just *did* remember. I

remembered so many things, but...

My eyes search his. I know I heard it. I know I did, but I...

"I can't remember," I tell him. Because none of those visions stayed. They felt so real, like they had to be remembered—those touches, those sounds, the feel of him—I had to be remembering the way he was with me, but they're gone now, just like the candle flame.

He strokes my hair back from my face. I can still taste the wine.

"Did you remember? For a moment at least?"

"I saw so many memories but they're all gone," I say, knowing he'll understand. "It's like a blur." I close my eyes and only a snippet comes back to me. My mind races and yet it's exhausted all at once.

"They'll come back."

"Something inside me..." I say, my eyelids growing heavy. "Something inside me does remember."

"You'll remember," he tells me. "We have all the time you need."

"It scares me," I tell him. What I've remembered is so much bigger than my life in Edinburgh and my life before. It's so much bigger than all the history I studied. This is unreal. It's like nothing I could have ever prepared for.

"There is nothing here to fear," he assures me, and I believe him.

I stare into his eyes before reaching my palm up to cup his stubbled jaw. I nearly say it, *I know I've loved you before*, but I don't. And as if he knows already, he kisses me right there, in that spot again and I moan, "Carlisle," as if I've said his name a thousand times before.

CHAPTER 8

APHRODITE

OLYMPUS

I stand before my altar, with its mirrors from the foot of the bath to the high ceiling. Its edges gilded and the edge of the water littered with rose quartz, vases of flowers, and candles whose flames reflect in the still water.

It's quiet, apart from the crackling of the fire, as I slip off the silk robe and step into the hot bath, enveloped by steam.

The entire entrance to my sanctuary is carved from aquamarine. It reflects the glimmers of the water so beautifully and the stone wraps itself onto the ceiling. The stones glimmer with otherworldly blues and golds running through them, shining into the water and making it appear as if it goes on forever.

When I close my eyes, the sirens call to me. There is so much love to be given and far too much taken for my liking.

I dip my fingers into the water and let the ripples on the surface settle before I sink my thoughts into it, following the path from past to present to future and back again until I find what I am looking for. What I need to see.

Who I need to see. Who needs me most for their highest self, I whisper as I stare into the flame that reflects in the mirror before me.

Persephone, my sister, is there in the water.

To my shock and confusion.

I recognize her form and her power as easily as I recognize that there is something wrong. I close my eyes and concentrate. Her doubt and fears of what is to come has plagued her, I know. But what I feel is darker. What is coming sends a chill down my spine. It is like nothing before.

Something has happened. Something has shifted.

It's as if a person might feel a creature under the water, lurking below, more powerful than a human and more deadly. Persephone's thoughts are dark like that, and as I concentrate harder, they begin to take a clearer form. The form is mostly a feeling, and that feeling is—

Cold.

It's the cold embrace of death. It's the cold from which mortals never awaken, and which they run from all their lives, whether they realize they're running from it or not.

I blink away the vision, but the chill still lingers on my skin. "She is a goddess," I whisper. Things of this nature should not be.

With the unsettled feeling I think of Ares. I need him now to ease this discomfort and fear of the unknown.

Glancing over my shoulder as if someone is there, I see nothing. Not my lover. The darkness though in the water remains when I think of Persephone.

I've never felt such things for a god.

I reach more deeply into it, trying to identify it. It reminds me of Ares, but it is not Ares.

It is another presence, close to Persephone. It is not an echo from the past or a possibility. It is someone near to her now, in the present moment.

My thoughts are disturbed as my sister enters my space, and I lose the connection to my power. Athena's bare feet pad on the quartz floor as she enters. It's still there, of course, but it's not as strong as it was, and I no longer sense the other presence as clearly.

As my sister crosses the floor, I try to keep my thoughts with Persephone for a few moments more.

It is not easy. The sound of Athena pulls me toward my physical form and away from the power in my basin. Athena cannot prevent me from using my power, but distractions make it more difficult.

She senses what I'm doing, of course.

Finally, Athena has had enough of waiting. She is not one known for patience.

She clears her throat, drawing a few steps closer, the hem of her long white dress dangerously close to the edge of the water. I do not know who the other presence was. Or—I can't be sure of who the other presence was. I have an idea, but I don't want to believe the evidence of my senses.

I will have to try again another time, when I can be certain I won't be interrupted.

"It is against all laws, what you are considering," Athena says, and Persephone floats away, her presence obscured from me, though I still feel the echoes.

I draw my fingers from the water and let the droplets fall from my fingertips back to the basin, allowing Athena to see that I have heard her words. I turn them over in my mind with the same kind of patience I hope to demonstrate for her. When I'm finished thinking, I fold my hands in front of me.

"Of whom are you referring?" I ask as if I don't know.

"Ivy. And her demon mate. It is unbecoming of you to meddle in the laws of the realm."

"She had thoughts of harm," I say. "I've done what I can to help her." They know me for beauty and selfishness, but it is the thoughts where I wish to dwell the most. "No one should ever wish for such things and the two of them together fixes that. It did not occur when she had her lover."

Athena scoffs. "A woman has thoughts of harm, and you gift her to a demon?"

I turn to my sister and stare her in the eyes. There is skepticism. We have spent many lifetimes being skeptical of each other's decisions. We see everything differently, but when I look at her, I try to see that she is my sister first and foremost.

"She has had thoughts of harming herself. You know I cannot allow that."

Athena narrows her eyes but a twinkle remains

on the surface. "Since when are mortal lives so precious to you? Sparta did not know such grace from you."

I hold her gaze for a few more long moments, then turn back to the basin.

The water is cold against my fingertips as I dip them back in and allow my consciousness to sink into it once again. It allows me to feel the woman's pain.

It's sharp and unrelenting, a sorrow that goes so deep it's almost as if she herself grew out of it. Almost as if she's always had this lump in her throat and this ache in her chest and an all-consuming sense of doom without him there. As if her soul knew he was missing.

My mind wanders with a reflection in the water once again. Persephone. A connection lies between them, and I cannot place it.

I do not know what it is, exactly, that pains her, because it is hidden in her mind, but it does not matter.

I'm not the only one who notices when things aren't balanced the way they should be.

"What plagues you now?" Athena asks, concern etched into her question.

"Persephone," I answer easily.

"You know she is changeable," Athena tries again. "The Fates cannot be sure of anything." My sister refers to the foretelling of Persephone losing her powers and living alone as a garden nymph...but that is not what lingers here.

"There is something else." I try to see it in the flames, but once again I am disturbed.

Athena lets out as sigh, shifting her weight from foot to foot to show me how unnecessary she thinks this is.

"She could've fallen for a mortal," Athena points out, bringing the conversation back to the deal I made with the demon. Her words cut through my thoughts, placed directly into my mind without her having to speak aloud. There are no vibrations in the air to disturb the water in the basin.

Athena sounds sure of herself. She always does. It's always right and wrong, black and white with my sister. "She *should* have fallen for a mortal. How were the gates opened between the realms?"

It's always rules with her.

The gates between realms are not to be opened. I merely allowed it for a moment.

I do not admit that to Athena, of course.

I choose to respond to the heart of what Athena has said, not the words themselves.

"You act as if demons are not worthy of love, sister," I say into her mind, not letting my voice carry into the water, either. "All are worthy. All should be loved. Even you."

I truly believe this. It is the guiding light that takes the most room in my heart. All should be loved. I may disagree about how this mortal or that goddess should be loved, but I know they must have it.

Athena's voice is cold. "I have love in what I do, who I am, and what I will be, and that is enough." Her choice not to take a lover is for her own.

"And I love you for that," I tell her, and the harshness softens in her expression.

"And I love you," she replies, begrudging sincerity in her tone. I haven't lied to her, and she knows this. "But you haven't answered my question. How did the portals to the underworld open?"

"Take it up with Hecate," I reply rather than admitting I signed the deal with Hades for his demon warrior. It was temporary and I can't imagine whatever shift Athena feels warrants any energy at all. "She should know and besides, the deal is done and it is over."

"The keeper of the keys and protector of the crossroads? As if Hecate would allow such things for a single love. She, of all gods, knows the comfort in grief."

The message underlying Athena's words is that she has no intention of asking Hecate about the gates and considers it a waste of her time to do so.

Good. Athena does not need to concern herself in matters that have passed.

I take several deep breaths and withdraw my fingers from the water. When I turn to face my sister again, I am holding nothing but love for her in my thoughts. I remind myself that all her contradictions serve a purpose in the parts we must play, and if Athena is to learn patience, it will have to be at her own pace, in her own time.

"Perhaps the old crone has love in her heart after all," I suggest. Stranger things have happened.

Athena faces me, her expression flat, until I go back to the basin.

As I sink into the water, I cannot help but think of the deal I made with Hades and the darkness in the water returns.

"I cannot help feeling something is off since the realm portals have opened—when they should have been sealed," Athena warns, and a chill goes down my spine.

That is the deal that allowed the realms to open.

If Athena knew the details of the agreement, her eyes would widen, then burn with anger, and I do not know how long our discord would last.

I cannot tell Athena and dismiss the thought from my mind as soon as it comes. I won't let the idea linger for even a few moments and won't entertain it as a real possibility.

"I mean the very thought that a demon could enter other realms...even Olympus... Does that not concern you?" she asks, and I swallow.

"Athena, please, do you not have other matters to tend to?" She scoffs at my question, leaving me alone in the room with my thoughts, the shift in the air, and her warning.

Hades would be a fool to come here. There's no chance he would dare show himself in Olympus.

The realization feels as though it strangles me. I felt him when I saw Persephone just a moment ago. It is him. What have I done?

And with that, I leave my sanctuary, in search of Ares.

Epilogue

Carlisle

Time blurs when it is endless. At least it does now that I have her.

Over and over again, she lets it fade into the background, and as the hours become days and the days become weeks, she stops thinking about the life she had without me and remembers those lives we lived together. The darkness and emptiness fade, and slowly we build our heaven together.

I've never felt so whole. It took not having her to know what pieces of me she filled. Little by little, the underworld has captivated her as it does me. No longer my hell, now that she is here by my side.

"There you are," she says one morning. It's the first thing I hear from her lips after she turns over and sees me lying next to her and *smiles.* "You're still here."

"Always."

Her curious mind has found peace here. So many books and stories to be told.

I've shown her everything I can that would bring her wonderment. I show her the river with stars beneath it and the mountain ranges that disappear into black clouds and the wide fields that have the darkest soil Ivy's ever seen. She stands up and closes her eyes, listening silently to the space around us, and finally opens them again.

We make new memories, like many of the things we shared before. Words we whisper into each other's ears. Promises we make under the covers at night.

Time has passed and our bond is stronger than ever, but still a thought plagues me.

"Are you content here with me?"

Her lips tilt into a soft smile as the fabric of her dress puddles around her. "Of course I am." She sits up on her knees, places both hands on my jaw, and kisses me before returning to the other end of the chaise.

"I was so afraid, and now I can't remember why." Ivy lounges on the couch, stretching her toes out so she can press them against my thigh. Her soft curves tempt me and the luxury of never needing or wanting anything but her is a comfort.

She's warm and soft and beautiful. The only woman I want to memorize like this. The only woman I craved so badly that I would have done anything to have her again. I would have done much worse things than I did to taste her sweet mouth even one more time. I would have done anything the gods asked of me.

I kiss her as much as I can. A hundred times a day. Two hundred. It doesn't matter. Every time I can put my lips to hers, I do it. I missed so many moments with her, and I'm not missing another one ever again.

"I love you Carlisle," she whispers, and a beautiful blush rises to her cheeks.

My heaven.

One day, not long after, her hand in mine, we walk down a path lined with onyx and dark flowers when a scream tears through the air.

A chilling scream. One that echoes in the air. Everything stops and the scream is all present. Her body presses to mine, her heart racing. "What was that?" she whispers.

In the distance, the life that exists is still. As if everything paused, wondering the same.

It was a sound from Hades's tower. Not from the hells beyond the wall.

It's a scream that should not exist. A goddess that does not belong here.

It was an act of war and the knowledge of my participation chills me to the core of my being. They will never know and I am to forget.

As Ivy needs to do as well.

"You didn't hear anything," I say just beneath my breath and then turn her around.

When Ivy looks up at me, her feet refuse to move. "I thought I heard someone scream."

"You didn't." I lean down and kiss her forehead, then tug her hand and continue walking down the path. She hesitates but follows. Her hand still in mine.

My heart doesn't stop beating frantically though.

I did it for her, I tell myself. I would do anything for Ivy.

Before we turn to our castle, I stop and steal a

surreptitious glance at the tower. No other screams come from that direction, and there's nothing in the windows that would be telling. The dark walls etched in the mountain of obsidian hide secrets, and I don't know why Hades has done what he has, but I know there will be consequences.

I bring the back of Ivy's hand to my lips and kiss her as if it could be the last. For a war among the gods could end us all.

About the Author

Thank you so much for reading my romances. I'm just a stay at home Mom and an avid reader turned Author and I couldn't be happier.

I hope you love my books as much as I do!

More by Willow Winters
www.willowwinterswrites.com/books

This is the Discreet Edition so no-one knows what you are reading.

You can find each edition at

www.willowwinterswrites.com/books

Made in the USA
Monee, IL
04 January 2025

76051728R00058